It's About
TIME!

Poems by
Florence Parry Heide
Judith Heide Gilliland
& Roxanne Heide Pierce

Illustrated by
Cathryn Falwell

Clarion Books
New York

Clarion Books
a Houghton Mifflin Company imprint
215 Park Avenue South, New York, NY 10003

Type is 16/20-point Garamond 3.
Illustrations are executed in mixed media collage.

Printed in Singapore.

Library of Congress Cataloging-in-Publication Data
Heide, Florence Parry.
It's about time! : poems / by Florence Parry Heide, Judith Heide Gilliland & Roxanne Heide Pierce.
p.   cm.
Summary: A collection of poems about the many aspects of time, including "The Time Machine,"
"Wasting Time," and "Time Zones."
ISBN 0-395-86612-X
1. Children's poetry, American. 2. Time—Juvenile poetry.
[1. Time—Poetry. 2. American poetry—Collections.] I. Gilliland, Judith Heide.
II. Pierce, Roxanne Heide. III. Title.
PS3558.E427177   1999
811'.54—dc21   98-7833
CIP
AC

TWP   10   9   8   7   6   5   4   3   2   1

IN LOVING MEMORY OF
FLORENCE FISHER PARRY

However much time we had,
it could never have been enough.

—*Your daughter and granddaughters*

For my time-challenged
family, with love

—*C.F.*

*I know what time is
until I am asked to explain it.*
—St. Augustine

Contents

IT'S HERE! IT'S HERE AT LAST!

—— *Announcing* ——

A spectacular event!

★★Free admission★★

ONE SHOW ONLY!

Never before! Never again!

★★★★★★★★★★★★★★★★★★★★★★★★★★★★★★★★★

Everyone welcome!

You'll love it! Don't miss it!

• • • • • • • • • • • • • • • • • • • •

AND HERE IT IS:

Telling Time

You've learned to tell time
so you know when to do
the things that you're supposed to do

time to get up
time to dress
time to clean your room, oh yes,
time for your programs on TV
time to be where you've got to be
time for school
time for bed
isn't it time your fish were fed?

Do this, do that,
just do, do, do!

Hey—you're not telling time—
it's telling you!

A Name by Any Other Name

This is the name of today:
     "Today."
I like that name, do you?
"Today" is what we'll call today
until the day is through.
And then we'll change its name, okay?
How does that sound to you?

We'll change its name to
        "Yesterday."
What else will we do?
Let's make
        tomorrow's
name
        "Today"!
Does that make sense to you?

The Time Machine

There was an inventor named Breen
who invented a Time Machine.
By mistake one time
he pressed rewind
and woke in his crib with a scream.

Time cut up in little pieces
years and months and weeks and days
time cut up in little pieces
time cut up in many ways

cut cut   chop chop   snip snip   tick tock

years and months and weeks and days

Days and hours, minutes, seconds

time cut up in many ways

cut cut   chop chop   snip snip   tick tock

time cut up and sliced so small

you hardly know it's there at all

14

Wasting Time

You know the rule: never waste time.
Use every single minute!
But I'm of the school where *squander*'s the rule;
in fact, I'm an honor roll student.

I fritter away the minutes and hours,
I excel in the art of inaction.
Each hour that passes and passes and passes
adds more to my sweet satisfaction.

EONS
MILLENNIUM
CENTURY
DECADE
YEAR
MONTH
WEEK
DAY
HOUR
MINUTE
SECOND
NOW
SECOND
MINUTE
HOUR
DAY
WEEK
MONTH
YEAR
DECADE
CENTURY
MILLENNIUM
EONS

The Measure of Time

By shadow, by star,
by sweep of the sun
or rising of the moon,
by tide, by earth's eternal turn,
we tell how time moves on.

Tick Tock Talk

"You tick me off," said the clock to the watch
as they passed the time away.
"You tock too much," the watch replied.
"Do you think we've got all day?"

Family Pictures

Looking through
some family pictures
I see a baby one of me—
that is me

but this is me—

now I wonder *which* is me?
The one that was,
the one that is,
or the one that's going to be?

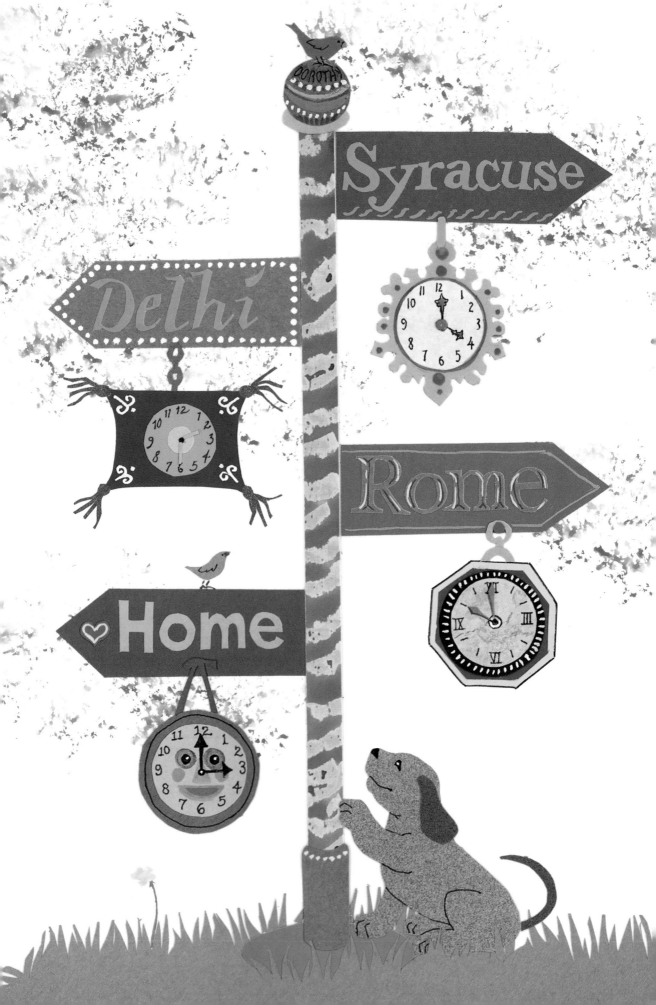

Time Zones

In Syracuse it's four o'clock,
it's half past two in Delhi.
It's ten in Rome and three at home—
but what time is it *really*?

Arrival

A very fast runner named Fay ran faster and faster each day.

She was very athletic and so energetic she arrived at tomorrow today.

Wasn't It Fun Tomorrow?

What do you think about having a party?
We could have it the night before last.
We'll invite all the friends we'll meet next year
before last week has passed.

The games we'll play! What fun they were!
Can't wait for the pizzas we ate.
And to think by the end of tomorrow
the party we had will be great!

Questions and Answers

When did time start?
    Long ago, long ago.
When will it end?
    We don't know, we don't know.
How long will it last?
    Forever and ever.
How long is forever?
    We'll never know, never.